Black Beauty

By Anna Sewell
Adapted by Cathy East Dubowski
Illustrated by Domenick D'Andrea

Bullseye Step into Classics™

Random House New York

Cover design by Fabia Wargin Design and Creative Media Applications, Inc.

A BULLSEYE BOOK PUBLISHED BY RANDOM HOUSE, INC.
Text copyright © 1990 by Random House, Inc.
Illustrations copyright © 1990 by Domenick D'Andrea.
Cover illustration copyright © 1993 by Thomas LaPadula.

Library of Congress Cataloging-in-Publication Data:
Dubowski, Cathy East. Black Beauty / by Anna Sewell ; adapted by Cathy East
Dubowski ; illustrations by Domenick D'Andrea. p. cm.–(Step-up classics)
SUMMARY: A horse in nineteenth-century England recounts his experiences
with both good and bad masters. ISBN 0-679-80370-X (pbk.)—
ISBN 0-679-90370-4 (lib. bdg.) 1. Horses–Juvenile fiction. [1.Horses–Fiction.]
I. Sewell, Anna, 1820–1878. II. D'Andrea, Domenick, ill. III. Title. IV. Series.
PZ10.3D8545B1 1990 [Fic]–dc20 89-62772

First Random House Bullseye Books edition: 1993

Manufactured in the United States of America   7 8 9 10

Contents

Chapter One

My First Home

The first place I can remember was a large pleasant meadow.

I lived on my mother's milk, as I could not yet eat grass. In the daytime I ran by her side. At night I lay close beside her. When it was hot, we stood in the shade of the trees. When it was cold, we slept in a warm shed near the master's house.

We were very fond of our master, Farmer Grey. He called my mother Duchess, and I think she was his favorite. He was a good kind man, so we were well off.

When I was old enough to eat grass, my mother went to work in the daytime. But she always came home at night.

There were six other young colts in the meadow. They were all older than I. Oh, how I loved to run with them! But sometimes they would bite and kick.

One day my mother told me, "The colts who live here are good colts, but they have not learned good manners.

"You come from a fine family. Your father has a good name in these parts, and I think you have never seen me bite or kick. So I hope you will grow up gentle and well-mannered. Do your work with a good will and never learn bad ways."

I never forgot my mother's words for I knew she had seen many things.

One day we heard the sharp cry of dogs.

"They have found a hare," said my mother. "Now we shall see the hunt."

A pack of howling dogs chased a frightened hare across the fields. Many men followed on horseback. The hare tried to get through our fence, but it was too late. The dogs were upon her.

One of the men rode up and whipped off the dogs. He held the hare up by the leg. She was torn and bleeding. All the gentlemen seemed pleased.

I did not know what to think!

Then there was a shout down by the brook. Two horses had fallen and thrown their riders. One man seemed all right, but the other man lay quite still.

"His neck is broken," said my mother.

The men ran to his side. I heard someone say it was Squire Gordon's only son.

Young Gordon's black horse lay moaning on the grass. A horse doctor came to look at him. He shook his head. "One of his legs is broken."

I saw a gun flash in the sunlight. There was a loud bang—and an awful shriek. Then all was still. The black horse moved no more.

My mother seemed very sad. The black horse's name was Rob Roy, she said. He was a fine bold horse whom she had known for years.

She never went to that part of the meadow again.

A few days later we heard the church bell ringing. They were taking young Gordon to the churchyard to bury him.

I never knew what they did with Rob Roy.

But it was all for one little hare.

Chapter Two

My Breaking In

In time I grew quite handsome. My coat was bright black, and I had one white foot and a pretty white star on my forehead.

When I turned four, my master said it was time to break me in. He would trust no one else to do it.

To *break in* means to teach a horse to wear a saddle and bridle and to carry a rider, or to pull a carriage. The horse must always do his master's will, even when he is tired or hungry.

11

So you see, this breaking in is a great thing.

First my master gave me some oats. He talked gently to me and petted me. Then he got the bit into my mouth.

Oh, it was a nasty thing! You cannot think how bad it felt. But I knew my mother always wore one when she went out, so I took it in good spirit.

Next came the saddle. It was not so bad. Then I had a few more oats and a little walk.

This we did every morning.

Then one day my master got on my back and rode me round the meadow. How strange it felt! But I was proud to carry my master.

The next day the blacksmith nailed a curved piece of iron to each of my hooves. My master called these *horse-*

shoes. They made my feet feel stiff and heavy, but in time I got used to them.

Then came the harness. A stiff heavy collar went round my neck, and a bridle held leather pieces called *blinkers* against my eyes. I could see only straight ahead.

Next was the saddle with a nasty stiff strap under my tail. That was the *crupper*. I never felt more like kicking, but of course I could not kick such a good master.

After that I often went out in double harness with my mother. With her it was easy to learn how best to go.

One day she told me, "There are many kinds of men in the world. Some are good and kind like our master, but others are bad and cruel.

"A horse never knows who may buy him, so I do not know where you will go. But I hope you will always do your best and keep up your good name."

I did not know it then, but I was soon to leave my first home.

Chapter Three
Birtwick Park

Squire Gordon bought me and took me to Birtwick Park. It was a pretty place with a large house and gardens. The stables had room for many horses and carriages.

I was put into a nice loose box with clean sweet hay. In a loose box the horse is not tied up but is left free to do as he likes. It is a great thing to have a loose box.

In the stall next to mine stood a fat gray pony. "How do you do?" I said. "What is your name?"

The pony turned round as far as he could. His was not a loose box, for he was tied up.

"My name is Merrylegs," he said. "I carry the young ladies on my back. Are you going to live next door to me? I hope you have a nice temper."

Just then a chestnut mare looked over at us. She was tied too. Her ears were laid back and her eyes flashed. "So! It is you who have turned me out of my box!"

"I have turned no one out," I said. "The man who bought me put me here." But she just turned away.

Later, when the mare went out, Merrylegs told me, "Her name is Ginger. She bites. One day she bit James Howard, our stable boy, in the arm and now the young ladies are afraid to come in here. I miss them very much. Maybe they will come again now, if you do not bite or snap."

"I never bite anything but grass, hay, and oats," I said. "I cannot think why Ginger does."

"It is just a bad habit," said Merrylegs. "But John Manly, our groom, does all he can to please her, and James is as kind as can be. So it is Ginger's own fault she did not stay in that box."

The next day John Manly brought me round for Squire Gordon to try. I remembered my mother's words and I tried my best to please him.

"How do you like him?" Mrs. Gordon asked when we came home.

"He is the most pleasant horse I have ever ridden!" said the squire. "What shall we call him?"

They thought of some names—Ebony, Blackbird—but those would not do. Then Mrs. Gordon said, "He is such a beauty, with his black coat and sweet face. What do you say to 'Black Beauty'?"

"Why, yes! That is just the name!"

John told James to call me Black Beauty.

"I might have named him Rob Roy," said James, "for I never saw two horses more alike."

"That's no wonder," said John. "Didn't you know? Farmer Grey's Duchess was the mother of them both."

So! Poor Rob Roy killed at the hunt was my brother! No wonder my mother was so sad that day. It seems horses have no family. At least, not after they are sold.

Chapter Four

Ginger's Story

A few days later I went out in the carriage with Ginger. I was surprised at how hard she worked. John never had to use the whip with us, and our paces were much the same.

On Sundays we were turned out into the orchard. What fun it was to run and roll in the soft grass! One quiet afternoon I told Ginger about my upbringing.

"My life has been so different," she said sadly. "No one was ever kind to me.

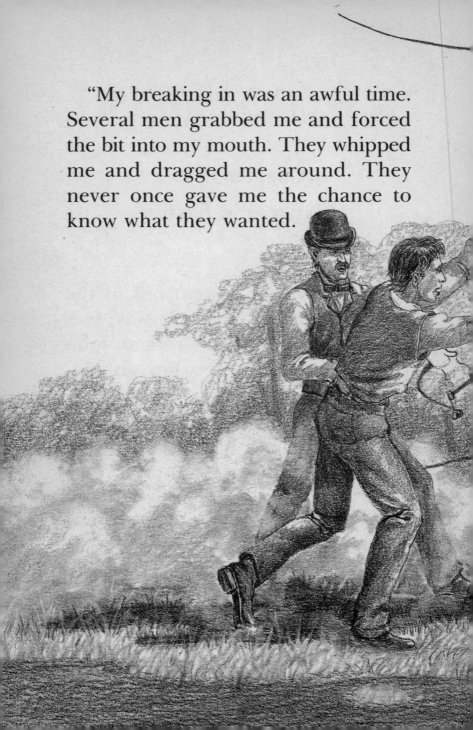

"My breaking in was an awful time.
Several men grabbed me and forced
the bit into my mouth. They whipped
me and dragged me around. They
never once gave me the chance to
know what they wanted.

"Then I was sold to a gentleman in London. He used the bearing rein to make me look fancy. I hated it worse than anything!

"Oh, I like to hold my head up as high as any horse, but a bearing rein makes you *keep* it up—for hours at a time.

"I wanted to please my master, but the bearing rein made me angry. To feel such pain just for the love of fashion!

"One day I could stand it no more. The rein was just too tight. I kicked as hard as I could till I broke free.

"My master sold me. After that I changed hands many times, but it was always the same. Each new master used the bearing rein, and each groom was meaner than the last. I made up my mind that men were my enemies.

"Of course, it is different here," said Ginger. "But who knows how long it will last?"

I was sorry for Ginger, but I knew very little then. I thought she made things out to be worse than they really were.

Then as the weeks went by, we became good friends. Ginger seemed happier and her temper grew sweet. Our lives at Squire Gordon's were very happy indeed!

"I do believe that mare is getting fond of me," said James one day.

"She'll be as good as Black Beauty soon," said John. "Kindness is all she wants, poor thing!"

Chapter Five

A Stormy Day

One day my master had a trip to make on business. John put me to the light cart, and we were on our way.

It had rained for days, and the wind was brisk. We rode along at a good pace till we came to a small wooden bridge.

"The river is rising fast!" the toll-keeper called out as we started to cross the bridge. "I fear it will be a bad night."

Soon we reached the town. The

master's business took a long time, and it was late when we started for home.

The wind was blowing harder now. The trees creaked and swayed, and leaves swirled round us as we quickened our pace. It was nearly dark when we came to the bridge.

As soon as my feet touched the wood, I knew something was wrong. I came to a dead stop.

"Go on, Beauty," said my master. He gave me a light touch with the whip, but I dared not go.

John got down and tried to lead me across. "Come on, Beauty. What's the matter?"

Of course I could not tell him, but I felt sure the bridge was not safe.

Just then the tollkeeper ran out of the house on the other side of the bridge. "Stop! The bridge is broken! If you cross, you will surely fall into the river!"

"Thank God!" said my master.

"That's my Beauty!" said John with pride.

We had to take a longer way home. Mrs. Gordon met us on the front steps. "Is everything all right, my dear?" she asked fearfully.

"Yes," said my master. "But only because your Black Beauty is wiser than we are. He kept us out of the river tonight."

What a good supper they gave me that evening! And such a thick bed of straw! There could be no better place than this, I thought, and I fell asleep feeling lucky indeed.

Chapter Six
The Fire

A few weeks later the master and mistress went to visit friends. James drove, for he was soon to go to a new place to work and needed the practice.

It was a long drive, so we had to stop for the night at a hotel. Ginger and I were left in the stable.

I cannot say how long I slept. When I woke up, it was still dark. I could hear Ginger coughing.

I heard another sound, too—a crackling sound. Above us flickered a strange red light. I did not know what it was, but it made me afraid.

The other horses woke up too. They pulled at their halters and they stamped the floor. Danger seemed all around us.

Outside I heard someone yell, "Fire!"

A young stableboy burst in with a lantern. His hands shook as he untied the horses. He tried to lead them out, but they would not move. He was in such a hurry—and seemed so scared himself. How could we trust him?

He tried to drag me out by force, but that only frightened me more.

Then I heard James's voice—as sweet and cheery as always. "Come, Beauty, come with me." He tied his scarf round my eyes. I could see nothing. There was only his calm voice. Only his gentle hands upon my neck. I let him lead me into the yard.

Then he slipped the scarf from my eyes and said, "Here, somebody! Hold this horse while I go back for the other."

I let out a shrill whinny when I saw him run back into the burning stable.

By now the hotel was in an uproar. People in nightgowns shouting and running! Frightened horses and carriages jammed into the yard!

My master pushed through the

crowd. He shouted toward the stable, "James! Are you in there?"

There was no answer—only a loud crash.

Then James ran out through the smoke, and he had Ginger with him!

"My brave James!" cried the master.

Ginger told me I had helped save her. "When I heard your whinny, I was no longer afraid to come out."

The whole stable was in flames as the fire engines clattered into the yard. James led us away from the smoke and the noise. But we could still hear the terrible shrieks of the horses trapped inside.

Chapter Seven

Going for the Doctor

"Well, James," John said when we were home again. "Guess who is going to take your place when you leave? Little Joe Green."

"Little Joe Green!" cried James. "He is just a child!"

"He is fourteen and a half," said John. "I was just as old when my parents died and the master took me in, so I am not one to turn up his nose at a little boy."

Soon after James left, the stable bell

woke me in the middle of the night. John came in, calling, "Wake up, Beauty! You must do your best. Tonight we ride for our mistress's life."

The air was frosty. The moon was bright. For eight miles I ran like the wind.

At last we came to the town. All was quiet but for the clatter of my feet upon the stones. The church clock struck three as we came to the doctor's door. John rang the bell twice and he knocked at the door like thunder.

An upstairs window flew open. The doctor was in his nightcap. "What do you want?" he called down.

"Mrs. Gordon is ill, sir!" called John. "Master says you must come or she will surely die!"

The doctor was soon at the front

door. "My son has taken my horse," he said. "May I have yours?"

John stroked my neck. I was very hot. "He has come at a gallop all the way, sir," said John. "But I guess there is no other way."

The doctor was not a good rider, but I ran my best. At last we were at Squire Gordon's front steps.

The doctor followed my master into the house. Little Joe Green was left to lead me to the stable.

I was glad to be home. My legs shook under me, and I was steamed and covered with sweat.

Joe rubbed me down, but he did not put my warm blanket on me, as he should have. He must have thought I was too hot.

Then he gave me a pail full of cold water. John would have given me something warm to drink. But I was so thirsty I drank it all. After that Joe gave me some hay and corn, and thinking he had done right, he went away.

Soon I turned deadly cold. I began to shake and I wished for my warm thick blanket. I wished for John, too, but he had eight miles to walk back from the doctor's house. So I lay down and tried to sleep.

After a long time I heard John at the door. I gave a low moan, for I was in great pain. In a moment he was at my side. He seemed to know just how I felt. He covered me with blankets and made warm gruel for me to drink.

"Stupid boy!" I heard him say to himself.

I do not know how long I was ill, but I thought I might die. I believe they all thought so too.

My master came to see me every day. "Poor Beauty!" he said. "Do you know you saved your mistress's life?"

How glad I was to hear that!

One night John was giving me some medicine when Joe's father, Thomas, stopped by.

"I wish you'd say a kind word to Joe," said Thomas. "He knows this was all his fault, but he is not a bad boy."

For a moment John did not speak. Then he said, "That horse is the pride of my heart. To think that his life might be lost like this! Still, I will try to give the boy a good word."

"Well, thank you," said Thomas.

"I am glad you see that it was only ignorance."

John's voice startled me as he shouted: "*Only* ignorance! Why, ignorance is the worst thing in the world, next to wickedness. People say, 'Oh, I did not know any better. I did not mean any harm.' They think that makes it all right."

I heard no more, for the medicine sent me to sleep. In the morning I felt much better. But I often thought of John's words when I came to know more of the world.

Chapter Eight
The Parting

I had now lived in this happy place three years. John had turned Little Joe Green into a fine young stable-boy. Ginger and I were the best of friends.

But sad changes were coming. Mrs. Gordon was often ill. The master lost his ready smile.

Then we learned our mistress must move to a warmer country. The news fell upon us like the ringing of a death bell. John went about his work without a word. Joe's whistle disappeared.

Dear Merrylegs was given to the vicar, who hired Joe to be his groom. Ginger and I were sold to an earl, who was an old friend of the master's. He thought we should have a good home there.

On the last day we drove our master and mistress to the train.

"Good-bye, John," Mrs. Gordon said. "God bless you!" John made no answer. Perhaps he could not speak. And poor Joe! He stood close by our heads to hide his tears.

The train puffed into the station and our master carried the mistress on board. Then the doors slammed shut and the train pulled away. We watched till there was nothing but a trail of thin white smoke.

"We shall never see her again," said John as he drove us slowly home. But, of course, it was not our home now.

The next morning Ginger and I were taken to Earlshall Park.

"There are no better horses anywhere," John told the groom, Mr. York. "But I must tell you. We never used the bearing rein with either of them."

"Well," said York, "they must wear the bearing rein here. I prefer the loose rein myself, and his lordship does not mind. But my lady insists on the latest style. The rein must be tight when she rides."

John shook his head. "I am sorry to hear that."

His good-bye to us was quick, and then he was gone. I never saw him again.

Chapter Nine
Earlshall Park

I had a new home, a new master—
and a new name. The earl wished
to call me Baron.

The very next afternoon Ginger
and I were put to the carriage. As
the clock struck three we were led to
the front of the house. Soon we
heard the rustle of silk as my new
mistress came down the steps. She
looked at us and did not seem
pleased, but she said nothing and got
in.

This was my first time wearing the

bearing rein. I could not put my head down when I wanted and I did not care for that. But it did not pull my head higher than I always carried it, so I did not mind too much.

The next day at three we were again at the door. We heard the silk dress rustle. "York!" cried my mistress. "Put those horses' heads higher! They are not fit to be seen!"

York shortened the rein. Now I began to understand why Ginger hated it.

That day we went up a steep hill. I had to pull with my head held high. How it strained my back and legs!

Each day York tightened the reins. I began to dread going out.

Then one day my lady came down late and the silk rustled more than ever. "York!" she cried. "Are you never going to get those horses' heads up? Raise them at once!"

York came to me first. He pulled the rein so tight, the bit cut my mouth. Then he turned to Ginger. She knew what was coming, so she began to kick with all her might. Suddenly she tripped over the carriage pole and fell down. York held her head to the ground till they could set me free.

They gave Ginger to the earl's son for hunting. She never went out with me again.

I cannot put into words the pain I knew for the next four months. I always came home tired and in poor spirits.

In my old home, I always knew that John and my master were my friends. But here I had no friends.

Chapter Ten
Reuben Smith

In the spring York drove the earl and his family to London. He left a man named Reuben Smith in charge.

I think everyone liked Smith. I know the horses did. But he had one great fault—the love of drink!

One day Smith rode me to town on business and left me in a stable. It was dark when he came back, and he was in a very bad temper. "Hurry up!" he shouted at the stableman who brought me out.

"Oh, look," said the stableman.

"Your horse has a loose nail in his front shoe. Shall I fix it before you go?"

"No!" cried Smith. "I haven't got time. It'll be all right till we get home." I thought it unlike him not to see about the shoe.

"Take care, then!" said the stableman as Smith climbed on my back.

Smith answered with a curse, and we galloped off into the dark night.

I went at my full speed, but still he whipped me. It was dark, the roads were stony, and my shoe grew looser with each step. Finally it flew off.

Smith should have known something was wrong, but he did not stop. That's when I knew he must be drunk—too drunk to care!

Soon my hoof was split to the

quick. The pain was too much to bear, and I fell hard upon both knees. Smith was thrown to the ground.

After a few minutes I got to my feet. Smith was lying by the road. He did not move.

It must have been midnight when I heard a horse's hooves. Then I heard Ginger—and men's voices.

"It's Reuben Smith!" cried one. "He's dead!"

"Why, the horse has thrown him!" said another. "Who would have thought the black horse would do that?"

Then they saw that I was hurt.

"Look!" said one. "His hoof is cut all to pieces. No wonder he fell! And look at his knees. Reuben must have been drunk to ride a horse over these stones without a shoe."

I shall never forget that painful walk home. It was more than three miles. At last I was led into my own box, and my knees were cleaned and wrapped in wet cloths. Then I lay down and tried to sleep.

The next day the horse doctor came to see me. "The horse is not spoiled for work," he said, "but he will never lose the scars on his knees."

I was turned into a small meadow to heal. I felt so free and the grass was sweet, but I was very lonely.

One morning the gate opened, and in trotted dear old Ginger! We were so happy to see each other. But she had sad news to tell.

The earl's son had ridden her too hard. Her strength was gone and her back was badly strained.

"So here we are—ruined in our youth," said Ginger. "You by a drunkard and I by a fool!"

Soon the earl came back from

London. He was very angry when he saw us. "What a waste!" he said to York. "The mare shall have a year's rest, but the black one must be sold. I will not have knees like that in my stables."

A week later I was put on a train and sent away.

Chapter Eleven
A Thief and a Fake

My new master was Mr. Barry. He knew little about horses, but he treated me well. My groom was named Filcher. He was gentle and knew his work. I should have had a good and easy place, but that was not to be.

For a few days all went well. My master ordered the best hay for me, with plenty of oats, crushed beans, rye grass, and bran. But each day I got fewer and fewer oats. This was troubling, because a horse needs oats for strength.

One day, about two months later, Mr. Barry rode me to visit a friend. The short easy ride tired me out.

"Your horse looks awfully thin," said the friend. "Is he getting enough to eat?"

"The best hay and oats money can buy!" said Barry.

The friend shook his head. "I can't say who eats your oats, but it is not this horse."

By now I knew where my oats went. Filcher's little boy came in every morning with an empty basket, and he always left with a basket full of my oats. They were stealing them! I heard them say why, too—to feed the chickens and rabbits the family raised to sell!

My master must have guessed what was going on. A few mornings later the boy left the stable with a basket full of oats. Minutes later a policeman came in holding the crying boy by the arm. "Now!" he said. "Show me where your father keeps his rabbit food."

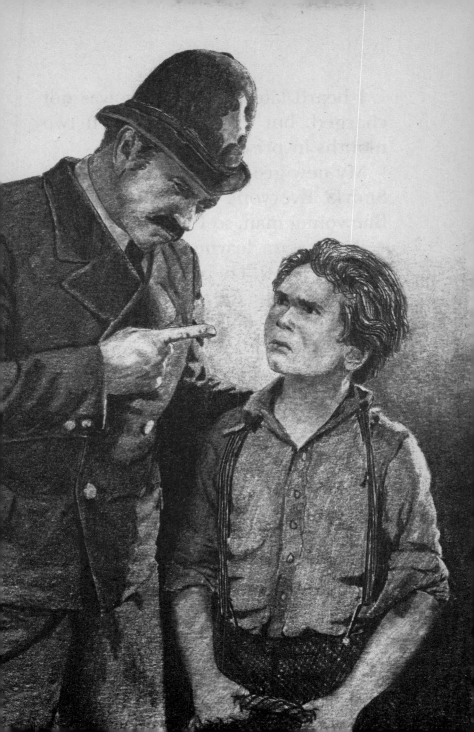

I heard later that the boy was not charged, but Filcher was given two months in prison.

My new groom was named Alfred Smirk. Everyone thought he was a fine young man, so I was full of hope.

But I soon learned he did things only for show. He brushed my mane and tail, but he did not clean my feet.

When he cleaned my box, he never took out all the hay. So under the new hay, there was always some wet rotting hay. It smelled awful, but that was not all. Standing on wet dirty straw made my feet sore.

One day my master drove me over some stones. My feet were so tender that twice I almost fell! Mr. Barry stopped at the horse doctor's to see what was wrong.

The doctor checked my feet and

shook his head. "Your horse has a bad case of thrush. I am surprised your groom did not see it before. We find this often in stables that are not kept clean."

Mr. Barry was so angry—cheated by two grooms! He gave up keeping a horse altogether. When my feet were well, I was sold again.

Chapter Twelve

A London Cab Horse

A horse sale must seem like a holiday fair to someone with nothing to lose, but it is no fun for a horse.

Many people came to look at me. They felt me all over and looked in my mouth. But those who were gentlemen always turned away when they saw my scarred knees.

Then one man stopped to make an offer. He was loud and harsh and I was afraid he would buy me.

But another man with kind gray

eyes offered more money, and I was his.

He fed me and saddled me, talking to me all the while. His name was Jeremiah Barker, he said. He was going to call me Jack.

Soon we were on our way. We drove along country roads, past fields, and through small villages. As darkness fell we came to the great city of London.

And what a place that was! People and horses and carriages everywhere! Streets to the right and streets to the left! I thought we should never stop.

Then we turned down a very narrow street. On one side stood a row of stables. The other side was lined with small, poor-looking houses. One of the doors few open, and out ran

Jeremiah's family—his wife, Polly, a boy named Harry, and a girl named Dolly.

Polly thought I was very handsome. The children petted me and pitied my scarred knees. I went to sleep thinking I was going to be happy at last.

Jerry had his own cab and another horse named Captain. Captain worked in the cab all morning, while I went out in the afternoon. Jerry was as gentle as John Manly, and he never used the bearing rein.

Still, my first week as a cab horse was hard, as I was not used to the noise and crowds of London. But Jerry was a good driver and soon we made a fine team.

Jerry would not work us on Sundays, even for the extra money. He said Sunday was a day of rest for all God's creatures.

Nor would Jerry drive me fast just because a gentleman was late for a party. Yet he once took me at top speed to carry a poor woman and her sick child to the hospital, and he did not charge her for the ride.

I grew quite proud of Jerry, and I think he was proud of me.

One day we were at a cab stand waiting for a fare. Many other cabs were there too.

A shabby cab drove up beside ours. The horse was a tired old chestnut. Her bones showed and her coat was dull. I tried not to stare.

I was eating some hay and the wind blew a small bit of it her way. She put her long thin neck down to pick it up. Then she looked round for more. She had such a hopeless look in her eye. I had the feeling I had seen her before. Then she looked at me and said, "Black Beauty, is that you?"

It was Ginger! But oh, how changed! I moved a step closer so we could talk. It was a sad story she had to tell.

She had been rested for a year at Earlshall Park, then sold to a gentleman. All was well till he rode her long and hard one day. That brought out her old back strain.

The gentleman sold her at once. In this way she changed hands many times. Each time was harder than the last. Each place broke her spirit more than before.

"My master says I am not worth what he paid for me," said Ginger. "He will work me hard till I am all used up."

I said, "In the old days you stood up for yourself when you were ill-used."

"True," she said. "But it is no use. Men are stronger than horses. All we can do is bear it on and on till the end. And I wish the end would come. I wish I were dead! I have seen dead horses. I am sure they feel no pain."

I was very much troubled. I put my nose up to hers, but I could say nothing to make her feel better. I think she was happy to see me, though. She said, "You are the only friend I ever had."

A few days later I saw a cart with a dead horse in it pass by. It was a chestnut mare with a thin neck. The head hung out of the cart and the eyes stared at nothing. I believed it was Ginger. I hoped it was, for then her troubles would be over.

Chapter Thirteen
Jerry's New Year

The Christmas season is a very merry time for most people, but it is no holiday for a cabman and his horse. So many people hurrying here and there! So many packages! The work is hard and often very late.

We spent many nights Christmas week standing in the snow and rain, and Jerry caught an awful cold. Each night his cough got worse. But the ladies and gentlemen dancing at the parties inside never seemed to think of us.

New Year's Eve we drove two gentlemen to a card party. They told us to come back at eleven. "Don't be late!" one of them said.

We drove up to the door again just as the clock struck eleven. Jerry was always on time. But no one came out, so we waited. The clock struck twelve, but still the door did not open.

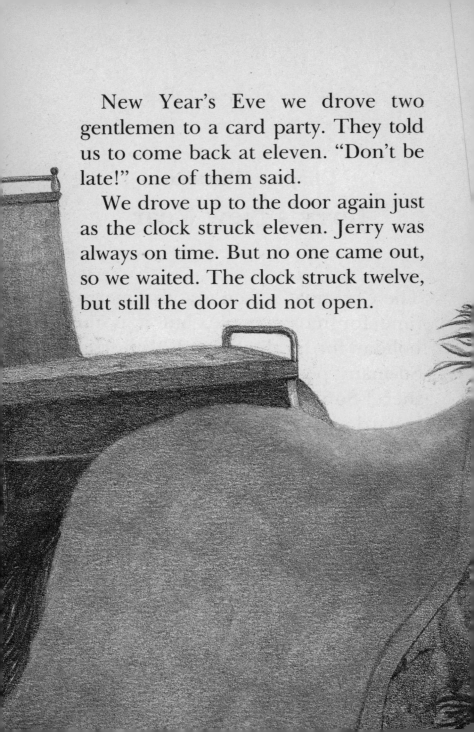

The night was icy cold, and it began to sleet. Jerry pulled my blanket round my neck. He stamped his feet to keep warm. The sound of his coughing seemed to fill the dark night. Still no one came.

It was a quarter past one when the two men came out. They said nothing about being sorry. Then we had to drive them nearly two miles in the cold.

At last we got home. Jerry's cough was worse, and he could hardly speak. Still, he rubbed me down and brought extra straw for my bed.

Late the next morning Harry came in and did Jerry's work without a word. Then Dolly came in crying and I heard them say their father was very sick.

There was no work for days. Only

the children came to the stable, as Polly would not leave Jerry's side.

In a week or two Jerry got a little better, but the doctor said he must never go back to driving a cab.

One day while Harry was working in the stable Dolly ran in, laughing. It was the first laughter I had heard in weeks.

"Harry!" cried Dolly. "Mother has had a letter from her old mistress. We are all to go and live with her. There is an empty cottage with a garden and a henhouse—and apple trees! Her driver is leaving in the spring. Father will be well by then, and he shall take his place!"

How wonderful it sounded! Then I learned I would not be going. The cab and the horses were to be sold.

This news broke my heart. I had

been happy with Jerry. What would happen to me now? After three years of cab work, I was no longer young and strong, and I could not hope for a better place.

On my last day Polly and the children came to say good-bye. "Poor dear Jack!" cried Polly. "I do wish we could take you with us."

Jerry still could not go out, so I never saw him again.

Chapter Fourteen
Hard Times

It was Jerry's wish that I should not go back to cab work, so I was sold to a corn dealer. Jerry thought I should have good food and fair work there.

It might have been so, but my master was not always around, and his foreman was hard on everyone. He always gave me twice more than I should carry. "Blackie can take it!" he would bark. "No use going twice when once will do."

Once again I was put on the bearing rein. In only a few months it broke my strength, so I could not do the work. They sold me—to be a cab horse again!

I shall never forget my new master. His voice was as harsh as cartwheels over gravel stones. His name was Nicholas Skinner.

Skinner owned cheap cabs and hired cheap drivers. He was hard on the men, and the men were hard on the horses. Here we had no Sunday rest—even in the heat of summer!

My driver had a cruel whip, and he whipped me often. I did my best and never hung back, but this soon took the heart out of me.

I began to understand how Ginger had felt. I began to wish that I would drop dead at my work. Only then could I be free.

One day my wish almost came true.

I had done a good day's work already when we picked up a family at the train station. You never saw so many bags and boxes!

"Oh, Papa!" said the man's young daughter. "I am sure this poor horse cannot carry all our things."

"Sure he can!" said my driver.

The load was heavy. I had not eaten or rested since morning. Still, I did my best till we came to a big hill. Then the bearing rein and the whip and all those boxes were too much. My feet slipped and I fell hard to the ground.

I could not move. Now I am going to die, I thought. All around me I heard voices as if in a dream. I heard the girl say, "Poor horse! It is all our fault!" Someone else said, "He's dead. He will never get up again."

I cannot say how long I lay there. Someone poured cold water on me and something warm was poured down my throat. At last I felt my life coming back. A kind man helped me to my feet. I was led to Skinner's stables and the horse doctor was called.

"This horse is not sick," said the doctor. "He has just been worked too much. Give him six months' rest. Then he may be able to work again."

"He can go to the dogs!" said Skinner.

"Well," said the doctor. "There is a horse fair in ten days. Rest him and feed him till then. You may get a little money for him there."

So for ten days I had rest and good food. I began to think it might be better to live after all.

Still, I was glad when it came time for the horse fair. Anything would be better than my life with Skinner. So I held my head up high and hoped for the best.

Chapter Fifteen

A New Beginning

At this horse fair I was put in with the old, broken-down horses. Many of the buyers and sellers did not look much better. Then I saw a kind-looking old man with a young boy by his side. His eye rested on me. I pricked up my ears.

"Look, Willie," the old man said to the boy. "There's a horse that has known better days. He might have been anything when he was young."

Willie stroked my face. "Poor fellow!" he said. "Could we not buy him? I am sure he would grow young in our meadows."

The gentleman laughed. "Bless the boy! He's as horsey as his old grandfather."

The old man looked me over. I stood as tall as my poor legs would hold me. He shook his head. But at last he drew out his purse.

Willie fairly danced with joy, and that seemed to make the old man happy.

My new master was named Mr. Thoroughgood, and he lived in a nearby village. He and Willie called me Old Crony, and they were so good to me. I had the best food and the run of the meadow every day. Soon I grew better in body and spirit. By spring I was well enough to pull a small cart.

"You were right, Willie, he's growing young," said Mr. Thoroughgood one day. "We must give him a little work now, and then we will find him a good home."

One day they cleaned me with extra care. Soon a man came to get me. At first he looked pleased. Then he saw my knees.

"I did not think you would sell my ladies an unsafe horse!" he said.

"Handsome is as handsome does," said Mr. Thoroughgood. "Try him. He is as safe as any horse you ever drove. If not, just send him back."

Chapter Sixteen

My Last Home

I was taken to a small, pretty house a mile or two from the village. Three sisters lived there. They would give me a week's trial.

The next morning their groom was cleaning my face, when he stopped and stared. "Why, that looks just like the star Black Beauty had! He is much the same height, too." He stood back to look me over. "White foot on the same side and a scar just there. Why, it must be Black Beauty!"

He looked into my eyes. "Beauty! Don't you know me? I'm Little Joe Green, the one who almost killed you!" He seemed overjoyed to see me.

I could not say that I remembered him, for he was grown now, with black whiskers and a man's voice. But I was sure he knew me and I was very glad. I put my nose up to him to tell him we were friends.

"Who broke your knees?" he said. "You must have had a bad time of it somewhere. But I shall see that you have a good time of it here."

In the afternoon he put me to a small cart, and one of the sisters, Miss Ellen, came out to try me. She was a good driver and seemed pleased with my paces. Joe told her he was sure I was Squire Gordon's old Black Beauty.

Back at the house, Miss Ellen's two sisters came out. She told them Joe's story. "I must write to Mrs. Gordon," she said. "When I tell her that her favorite horse has come to us, how pleased she will be!"

The ladies drove me every day for a week and saw that I was quite safe. Of course they would keep me, they said, and they would call me by my old name.

Black Beauty! I had been called so many different things. How good it felt to hear my old name again!

I have now lived in this happy place for a year. My work is easy, and Joe is the kindest of grooms. I feel my strength and my spirits returning.

My ladies promise I shall never be sold, so I have nothing to fear. I am home, and here my story ends.

But sometimes, before I am quite awake, I fancy I am still at Birtwick Park. And I dream I am standing beneath the shade trees, talking with my old friends.

Cathy East Dubowski believes that anyone who has ever looked an animal square in the eye knows that all animals have hearts and souls—just like people. Besides, her dog Falstaff told her this was true. Ms. Dubowski is a freelance editor and writer whose children's books include the Random House Step into Reading™ titles *Pretty Good Magic* and *Cave Boy*, illustrated by her husband, Mark Dubowski. She lives in North Carolina with Mark and their daughter, Lauren.

Domenick D'Andrea has illustrated covers for many history and adventure books. He specializes in illustrating stories about the West—especially horse stories. Mr. D'Andrea lives in Stratford, Connecticut.